"The CD...has been picked up by institutions such as the Bronx Zoo, The Children's Museum of Long Island, and the American Museum of Natural History—a strong indication of its educational worth."
    -*Big Apple Parent*

"...Music to entice youngsters to practice their listening and rhyming skills while singing along to zippy tunes..."
    -*Parenting Magazine*, "Parenting Pick"

"The Guess Who Zoo is an original, fully engaging, and enthusiastically recommended entertainment with 'fill in the blank' musical guessing games..."
    - The Midwest Book Review, "The Music Shelf"

AUDIENCES

"*The Guess Who Zoo* was a great success at our Bring Your Kids to Work Day. Parents had as much fun as the kids did!"
    -Vanessa Vega, Human Resources, Giorgio Armani

"...an incredibly popular event that brought record visitors to the museum..."
    -Andrea Donnely, Children's Museum of the Arts
    (SoHo, NYC)

"The performance was not only fun, but educational, too...parents are still telling me how much their children enjoy listening to the CD we gave away as party favors."
    - Sarah Sternklar, PhD (NYC)

Fondly remembering Arlene who loved reading poetry to our children and grandchildren—and always paused to let them guess the rhymes.

-Howard Eisenberg

Guess Who Zoo

Story © 2013 by Howard Eisenberg

Requests for permission to excerpt or make copies of any part of the work should be submitted online at info@mascotbooks.com or mailed to Mascot Books, 560 Herndon Parkway #120, Herndon, VA 20170.

PRT0213A

Library of Congress Control Number: 2012955274

Printed in the United States

ISBN-13: 9781620861745
ISBN-10: 1620861747

www.mascotbooks.com

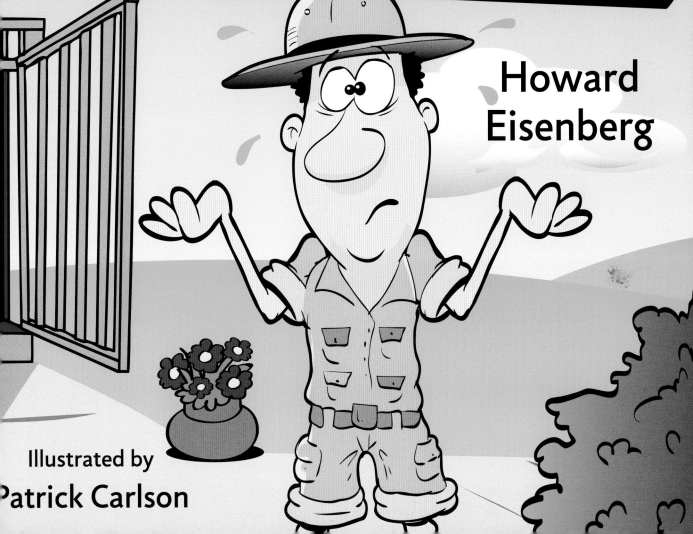

The Zookeeper was fast asleep.
He woke up in a stew:
"Good heavens, someone stole my keys.
How can I guard my zoo?"

He spied a note attached nearby
Tacked there upon a tree:
"I took your keys and freed my friends."
It was signed: "The Monkey."

A postscript followed and it said,
"We like this zoo the best,
But we will not return until
All of our names are guessed."

"So will you do this for us?"
An impatient lion roared:
"We really need some fun.
We've all been kind of bored."

The monkey called down from the tree:
"Please play our guessing games!"
Said Zookeeper, "That's silly.
I already know your names."

The monkey paused. "You're right," he said.
"But children love to play.
Ask them to do the guessing.
You'll get back your keys today."

"Okay, okay," said Zookeeper.
"Kids, please take center stage.
Get ready to start guessing.
It's time to turn the page."

Are you ready to start?

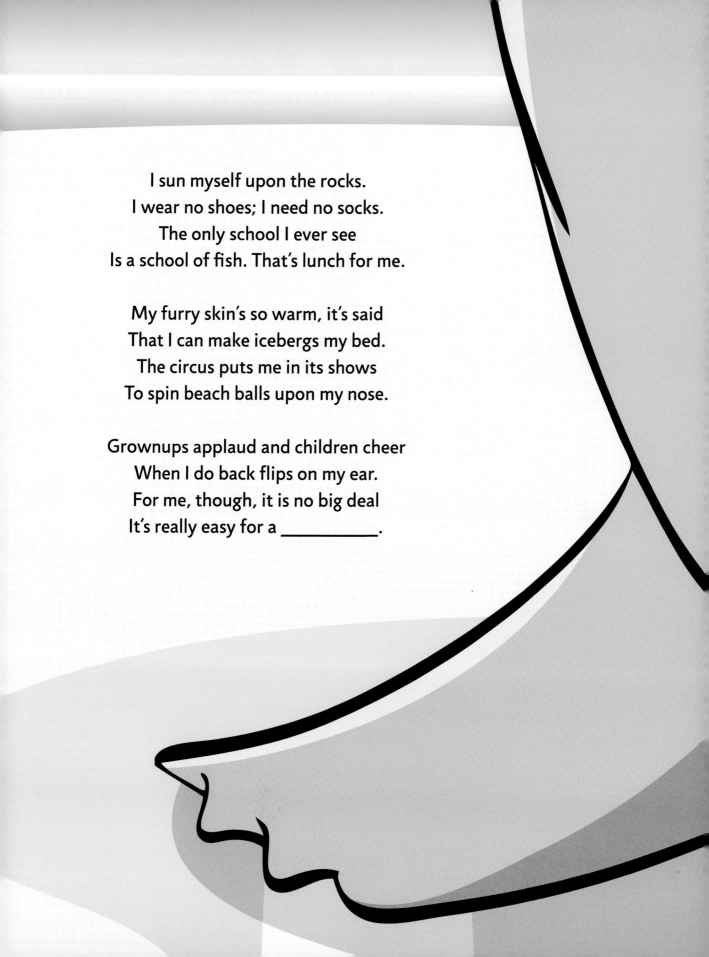

I sun myself upon the rocks.
I wear no shoes; I need no socks.
The only school I ever see
Is a school of fish. That's lunch for me.

My furry skin's so warm, it's said
That I can make icebergs my bed.
The circus puts me in its shows
To spin beach balls upon my nose.

Grownups applaud and children cheer
When I do back flips on my ear.
For me, though, it is no big deal
It's really easy for a _____.

SEAL

Toss me a fish. I could use a good meal.
Gratefully yours. Your friend the seal.

When I'm not dozing in the ooze,
The river's where you'll see me cruise.
Upon my face, a crooked smile,
Much like my cousins on the Nile.

I fish with neither rod nor reel.
Upon my finny friends, I steal.
My jaws gape open very wide;
One gulp—ten fish disappear inside.

Frogs and wading birds unwary
Are mangled by my molars scary.
Alas, I don't know wrong from right
When overwhelmed by appetite.

In fact (please do not tell their maters),
My favorite dish is baby gators.
When hunger's gone, I'm very peaceful,
Sunbathing in my skin so creaseful.

Feeling safe from any fate,
Who wouldn't dressed in armor plate?
Where buzzards glide and skeeters sting
In swampy Everglades, I'm king.

Believe me, there is no one greater
I'm the mighty _____ .

ALLIGATOR

Gonna take a swim. I'll see you later.
Your scary friend the alligator.

My coat is bright and speckled.
My favorite lunch is leaves.
I daintily nibble down below
Or high on the tallest trees.

My neck is as long as a light pole.
It makes little children laugh.
When I stretch it out to lick your hand,
You'll know I'm the _____.

GIRAFFE

Would you like my autograph?
I'll gladly sign it the giraffe.

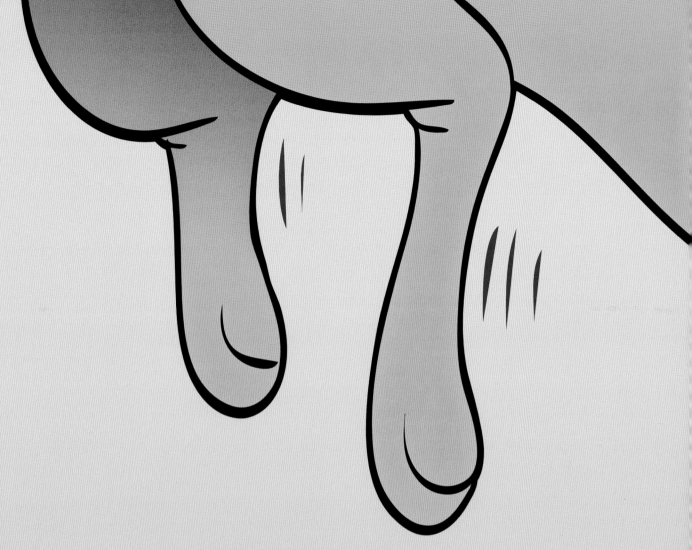

I look like a rabbit six feet tall.
I'm a great kick boxer. I kick. You fall.
My joeys (well, babies) sleep in my pouch.
It's soft and comfy as your mother's couch.

My strong hind legs give me lots of power;
I can leap ten feet to nibble a flower.
I run as fast as a motor car;
Forty miles an hour can take me far.

Are you ready to guess?
Well, I've one more clue.
I come from Down Under
I'm a _____ .

KANGAROO

Oh, very good! I knew you knew
I'm an Australian kangaroo.

From early spring to autumn,
Through the wild greenwoods I wind
Eating nuts and roots and candy bars
That hikers leave behind.

Where flowers bloom and bees buzz 'round,
I smile, not 'cause they're funny.
I smile because they'll lead me to
A beehive full of honey.

My fav'rite snack, I doubt you'd like.
I find it when it's colder
A tasty cake of frozen ants
Concealed beneath a boulder.

When winter winds begin to howl
And snowflakes fill the skies,
I pick myself a cozy cave,
Crawl in, and close my eyes.

I hibernate all winter
In my furry underwear,
'Cause without my summer berries,
I'd be hungry as a _____.

BEAR

I'm Brown, Black, and Polar. Increasingly rare
Please save some wild spaces for your friend the bear.

Bananas are my favorite lunch.
I peel and eat them by the bunch.
The jungle is my habitat.
For me friends, that is where it's at.

I love to swing from tree to tree.
I do it quite dramatically.
One reason that I never fail
Is what's called my prehensile tail.

If I miss and start to fall,
I grab a branch with it, that's all.
I'm brave, athletic and quite spunky
And yes, mischievous as a _____.

MONKEY

I'm very nimble. Never clunky.
I'm sure you've guessed that I'm the monkey.

Thirst is never a problem;
It doesn't make me a grump.
I manufacture water
From the fat inside my hump.

When I spy an oasis,
I gallop there pell-mell.
If my master didn't stop me,
I'd drink the whole darned well.

I can travel for days
Beneath bright blazing skies.
I'll eat thistles and thorns
If I can't find date pies.

I'm positively glamorous
With eyelashes oh so long.
They keep the sand out of my eyes
Where it certainly doesn't belong.

I'm the ship of the desert,
A remarkable mammal.
There's no doubt
That I am the _____.

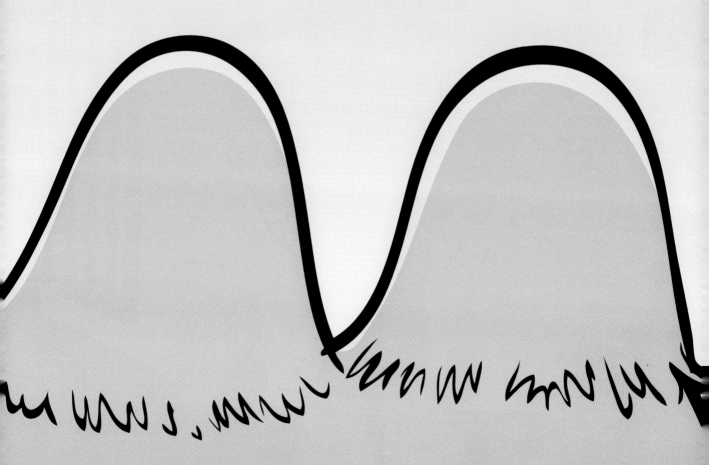

CAMEL

Should I paint my toenails in red enamel?
That would make me an even more gorgeous camel.

No animal is strong as I.
Watch me uproot that tree!
My ten-pound brain never forgets.
Want to test my memory?

My teeth (well, tusks) grow ten feet long.
I seldom get a cavity.
When I nap, they prop me up,
Defying gravity.

My skin is thick. Almost an inch.
My trunk's as long as a man.
Could I wrestle six gorillas?
I've no doubt that I can.

Rajahs in howdahs rode my back,
Tiger-hunting from their litters.
Now tigers are as rare as I.
We are both endangered critters.

Someday I'll go home to the jungle,
But not right now. I can't.
I'm much too busy being
A circus _____.

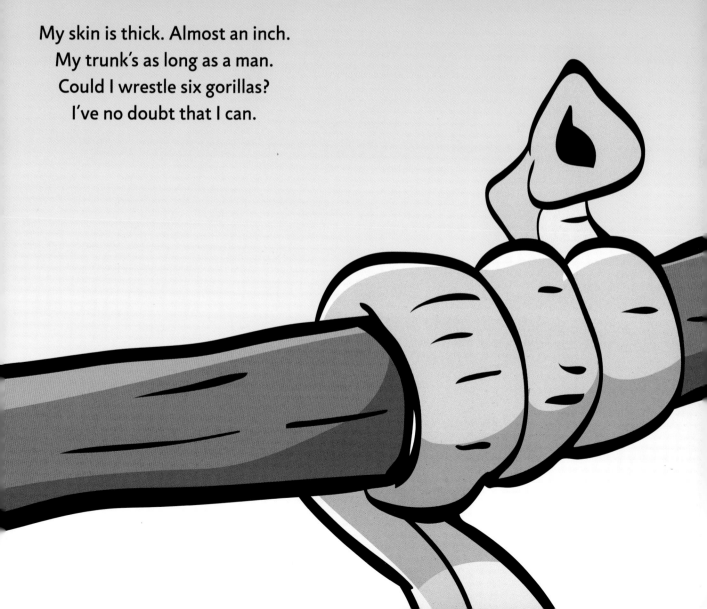

ELEPHANT

Gee, friend. You are the very best
You aced another guessing test.

When I am born, I weigh a ton.
Well, almost. Birthing me's no fun.
Built like a tank. My hide is thick.
It keeps germs out. I'm rarely sick.

I stroll the bottom of the river
Where tasty water grasses shiver.
A thousand fishes flee in fright;
They fear my awesome appetite.

They need not worry. All I want
Is tasty underwater plants.
I'm bulky as a baby grand,
But you should see me race on land.

My swift squat legs look mighty slow,
But I can catch 'most any foe.
I really only look ferocious;
You're quite safe from my jaws atrocious.

I'd rather wallow in the mud,
Dreaming of heavy rains and flood.
You say that I'm a what-amus?
Nope. I'm the _____.

HIPPOPOTAMUS

Truly awesome! You impressed me
With how quickly that you guessed me.

Everybody thinks it's gross
That I eat creepy-crawly things,
But I find that they're delicious,
Even the kind that stings.

I eat a thousand for a snack
And more if I can find them.
I'm absolutely toothless,
So I let my stomach grind them.

When I find a mound, I stop for lunch.
My keen claws dig a tunnel,
I thrust my two-foot tongue inside,
Form a long and sticky funnel.

What a tasty meal those dear ants make.
It couldn't be any sweeter.
Then it's nap time in a hollow log
For this tummy-full _____.

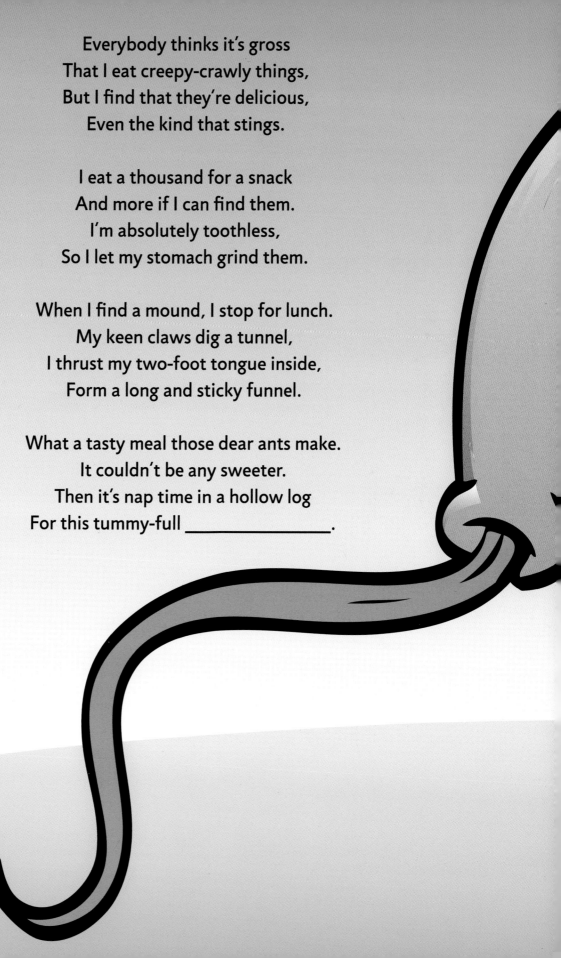

ANT EATER

Yippee! An anthill! Life couldn't be completer.
It brings endless joy to this starved anteater.

My face is quite adorable,
But you may think it horrible.
I wear a mask upon my eyes.
Why not? I came to rob you guys.

When sun has set and darkness falls,
I want spaghetti and meatballs.
Since I do not know how to cook,
Your garbage can is where I look.

My nose can sniff from half a mile.
When it smells leftovers, I smile.
The stuff you left upon your platter,
I'll dine upon with midnight clatter.

I lick my lips and thank your Mommy
For chicken nuggets and salami.
Oh how I feast beneath the moon!
I'm sure you know my name:

_____.

RACCOON

I'm singing a very happy tune
'Cause, well, you guessed my name raccoon.

"You've done it, kids!" the Monkey cried.
"Zookeeper's been depressed,
But now I can return his keys
'Cause all our names are guessed.

I hope you'll read this book again
And this won't be the end.
Please come and read me anytime.
I'll always be your friend."

IF ANIMALS COULD TALK...

Arctic water's really cold. But blubber under my skin keeps me warm as whole wheat toast.

We come in all sizes – from a 50-pound Galapagos seal to a 2-ton Elephant Seal.

Our whiskers aren't just handsome. They vibrate for hunting ("Yum!") delicious fish.

But, alas, sharks and polar bears think I'm delicious, so they hunt me.

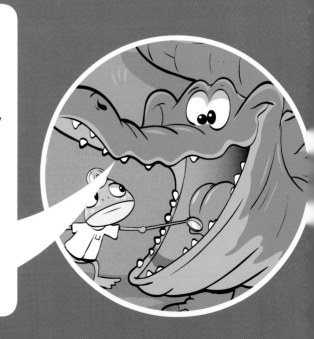

We've been around 200 million years. (Modern humans? You're newcomers.)

Who needs dentists? Lose a tooth? I grow a new one. 2,500 in a lifetime.

Can you tell a gator from a croc? My head is rounded. Crocs' are V-shaped.

What do the U.S. and China share? (Right! Sesame noodles and alligators.)

I'm the tallest animal in the world.
(Well, dinosaurs were, but they're extinct.)

Lions fear me. One good kick from my sharp hooves and they go flying.

Zebras and wildebeests know that, so they like to graze near me.

Acacia tree leaves are my favorite snack. I eat 70 pounds a day -- thorns and all.

I was born the size of an almond. Growing in Mom's pouch, I'm called a Joey.

Her pouch is waterproof, so Mom can swim without drowning me.

We're certainly not in the Mafia, but a group of us is called a mob.

I can't walk backwards. (Neither can emus.) So I never retreat.

Slow and clumsy? Not bears. Some of us run fast enough to catch a horse.

When Theodore Roosevelt refused to shoot a cub, the Teddy Bear was born.

My curved claws make tree climbing easy for a brown bear like me.

Why do I hibernate all winter? Food's hard to find. I might as well sleep.

If I yawn, it means back off! It's a warning that I'm getting angry.

If you were a monkey's uncle, you'd never catch cold. Monkeys never do.

If I'm only as big as your dad's hand, I'm a pigmy marmoset monkey.

Sure I like bananas. But I never eat their peels. (Would you?)

I can drink a bathtub full of water. Two if I'm really thirsty.

In Arabic, my name means "beauty." (Sounds right to me.)

Most horses stand when they're sleeping. I'm smarter. I lie down.

If I don't like you, I spit a stinky fluid all over you. ("Quick! Duck!")

Mama hippos give birth under water. (Good thing I'm born knowing how to swim.)

My webbed toes act like paddles to help me swim.

I see approaching danger even when submerged. My eyes are on top of my head.

I can't walk on water, but I can walk and graze on the river bottom.

I make rounds. On a good day, I dine at more than 100 ant and termite nests.

I never eat a whole ant colony. (I leave the rest for another meal.)

I'm toothless, but my sharp claws are so powerful even jaguars fear me.

When I eat ants, my tongue flicks in and out like lighting --100 times a minute.

Surprise! I don't really like peanuts. (So don't throw me any.)

It takes me almost two years to make a baby. (But I sure do make big ones.)

I throw sand on myself to avoid sunburn. (Gosh, I can't afford Sun Block.)

I like looking in mirrors. Like apes (and like you), I recognize myself.

I often live in the hollow of an old oak tree. (Not beech. Too smooth. Hard to climb.)

My flexible paws easily pry lids off garbage cans. (Oh boy! I smell French fries.)

I'm great at fishing. (My paws and claws are as good as your dad's fishing rod.)

I'll eat anything that won't eat me: fruits, nuts, veggies, insects, even a tasty mouse.

Howard Eisenberg's light verse has appeared in *Parenting Magazine*, *Baby Talk*, and *The Wall Street Journal*, but he wrote his first Guess Who Zoo poems at 30,000 feet on postcards to his grandchildren. They were penned on a Qantas jet while sitting beside his late wife, Arlene (co-author of the *What to Expect* parenting series) during a book and zoo tour of Australia and New Zealand. Suggested Arlene, "Why not collect the postcard poems into a children's book?" Now that's where they are-with more to come as part of this series in *Guess Who Farm* and *Guess Who Neighborhood*.